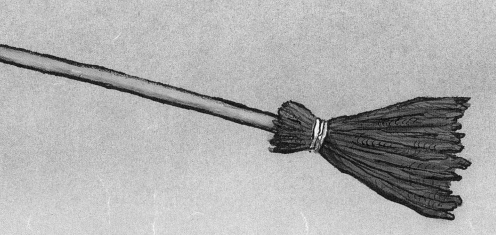

For Natasha, Sabrina and Jasmine—J.D.

First published in the United States
by Dial Books for Young Readers
A division of Penguin Putnam Inc.
345 Hudson Street
New York, New York 10014

Published in Great Britain
by Macmillan Children's Books
Text copyright © 2001 by Julia Donaldson
Pictures copyright © 2001 by Axel Scheffler
All rights reserved / Printed in Italy
7 9 10 8

Library of Congress Cataloging-in-Publication Data
Donaldson, Julia.
Room on the broom / by Julia Donaldson ; pictures by Axel Scheffler.
p.   cm.
Summary: A witch finds room on her broom for all the animals that ask for a ride,
and they repay her kindness by rescuing her from a dragon.
ISBN 0-8037-2657-0
[1. Witches—Fiction. 2. Animals—Fiction. 3. Dragons—Fiction. 4. Stories in rhyme.]
I. Scheffler, Axel, ill. II. Title.
PZ8.3.D7235 Ro 2001   [E]—dc21   00-045182

Room on the Broom

by Julia Donaldson

pictures by Axel Scheffler

DIAL BOOKS FOR YOUNG READERS NEW YORK

The witch had a cat
    and a hat that was black,
And long ginger hair
    in a braid down her back.
How the cat purred
    and how the witch grinned,
As they sat on their broomstick
    and flew through the wind.

But how the witch wailed
    and how the cat spat,
When the wind blew so wildly,
    it blew off the hat.

"Down!" cried the witch,
     and they flew to the ground.
They searched for the hat,
     but no hat could be found.

Then out of the bushes
     on thundering paws
There bounded a dog
     with the hat in his jaws.

He dropped it politely,
   then eagerly said
(As the witch pulled the hat
   firmly down on her head),
   "I am a dog, as keen as can be.
   Is there room on the broom
   for a dog like me?"

"Yes!" cried the witch,
   and the dog clambered on.
The witch tapped the broomstick and
   whoosh! they were gone.

Over the fields and the
    forests they flew.
The dog wagged his tail
    and the stormy wind blew.
The witch laughed out loud
    and held on to her hat,
But away blew the bow
    from her braid—just like that!

Then out from a tree,
   with an ear-splitting shriek,
There flapped a green bird
   with the bow in her beak.
She dropped it politely
   and bent her head low,
Then said (as the witch

"D own!" cried the witch,
   and they flew to the ground.
They searched for the bow,
   but no bow could be found.

tied her braid in the bow),
"I am a bird,
        as green as can be.
Is there room on the broom
        for a bird like me?"

"Yes!" cried the witch,
        so the bird fluttered on.
The witch tapped the broomstick and
        whoosh! they were gone.

Over the reeds and the
    rivers they flew.
The bird shrieked with glee
    and the stormy wind blew.
They shot through the sky
    to the back of beyond.
The witch clutched her bow—
    but let go of her wand.

"Down!" cried the witch,
    and they flew to the ground.
They searched for the wand,
    but no wand could be found.

T hen all of a sudden
        from out of a pond
Leaped a dripping wet frog
        with a dripping wet wand.
He dropped it politely,
        then said with a croak
(As the witch dried the wand
        on a fold of her cloak),
"I am a frog, as clean as can be.
Is there room on the broom
        for a frog like me?"
"Yes!" said the witch, so the frog
        bounded on.

The witch tapped the broomstick and
        whoosh! they were gone.
Over the moors and the
        mountains they flew.
The frog jumped for joy and . . .

THE BROOM
SNAPPED IN TWO!

Down fell the cat and the dog
and the frog.
Down they went tumbling
into a bog.

The witch's half-broomstick
flew into a cloud,
And the witch heard a roar
that was scary and loud . . .

"I am a dragon, as mean as can be,
And you, witch, look like
   a good supper to me!"
"No!" cried the witch,
   flying higher and higher.
The dragon flew after her,
   breathing out fire.
"Help!" cried the witch,
   flying down to the ground.
She looked all around
   but no help could be found.

The dragon drew nearer and
   started to drool.
He said, "I won't let you go—
   do you think I'm a fool?"

B ut just as he planned
    to begin on his feast,
From out of a ditch
    rose a horrible beast.
It was tall, dark, and sticky,
    and feathered and furred.
It had four frightful heads,
    it had wings like a bird.
And its terrible voice,
    when it started to speak,
Was a yowl and a growl
    and a croak and a shriek.
It dripped and it squelched
    as it strode from the ditch,
And it said to the dragon,
    "Buzz off!–
    THAT'S MY WITCH!"

The dragon drew back
and he started to shake.
"I'm sorry!" he spluttered.
"I made a mistake.
It's nice to have met you,
but now I must fly."
And he spread out his wings
and was off through the sky.

Then down flew the bird
and down jumped the frog.
Down climbed the cat,
and, "Phew!" said the dog.
And, "Thank you, oh, thank you!"
the grateful witch cried.
"Without you I'd be
in that dragon's inside."

Then she filled up her cauldron
and said with a grin,
"Find something, everyone,
throw something in!"
So the frog found a lily,
the cat found a cone,
The bird found a twig,
and the dog found a bone.

They threw them all in
and the witch stirred them well,
And while she was stirring,
she muttered a spell.
"Iggety, ziggety, zaggety, ZOOM!"

Then out rose . . .

A TRULY MAGNIFICENT BROOM!

With seats for the witch
  and the cat and the dog,
A nest for the bird and
  a pool for the frog.

"Yes!" cried the witch,
  and they all clambered on.
The witch tapped the broomstick and
  whoosh! they were gone.